Copyright © 1967, renewed 1995 by Random House, Inc. All rights reserved. Published in the United
States by Golden Books, an imprint of Random House Children's Books, a division of Random House, Inc.,
1745 Broadway, New York, NY 10019. Originally published in 1967 by Western Publishing Company, Inc.
Golden Books, A Golden Book, and the G colophon are registered trademarks of Random House, Inc.
www.goldenbooks.com
www.randomhouse.com/kids
Educators and librarians, for a variety of teaching tools, visit us at www.randomhouse.com/teachers
Library of Congress Control Number: 2008921146
ISBN: 978-0-375-84964-0 (trade)   978-0-375-96964-5 (lib. ed.)
PRINTED IN CHINA
10 9 8 7 6 5 4 3 2
First Random House Edition 2009

Never Talk to Strangers

By Irma Joyce

Illustrated by George Buckett

A GOLDEN BOOK • NEW YORK

If you are hanging from a trapeze
And up sneaks a camel with bony knees,
Remember this rule, if you please—
Never talk to strangers.

If you are shopping in a store
And a spotted leopard leaps through the door,
Don't ask him what he's shopping for.
    Never talk to strangers.

If the doorbell rings, and standing there
Is a grouchy, grumbling grizzly bear,
Shut the door. Your mother won't care.
Never talk to strangers.

If you are in the park for a walk
And out of a cloud parachutes a hawk,
Unless you know his name, don't talk.
Never talk to strangers.

If you are waiting for a bus
And behind you stands a rhinoceros,

Though he may shove and make a fuss,
Never talk to strangers.

If you are out for a mountain climb
And a coyote asks if you know the time,
Let him wait for a clock to chime.
Never talk to strangers.

If you're mailing a letter to Aunt Lucille
And you see a car with a whale at the wheel,
Stay away from him and his automobile.
    Never talk to strangers.

If you are riding your bike at noon

And you see a bee with a bass bassoon,

Don't stop to ask the name of his tune.
Never talk to strangers.

If you are swimming in a pool
And a crocodile begins to drool,
Paddle away and repeat this rule—
Never talk to strangers.

But . . . if your father introduces you
To a roly-poly kangaroo,
Say politely, "How do you do?"
    That's not talking to strangers,
    Because your father knows her.

If your teacher says she'd like you to meet
A lilac llama who's very sweet,

Invite her over and serve a treat.
That's not talking to strangers,
Because your teacher knows her.

If a pal of yours you've always known
Brings around a prancing roan,
Welcome him in a friendly tone.

That's not talking to strangers,
Because your pal knows him.

If while eating toast and honey,
You catch a glimpse of the Easter Bunny,

Tell him a joke. He'll think it's funny.
That's not talking to strangers,
Because *everyone* knows him.

Now I'll tell you why you've never heard
This jolly giraffe say a single word.
It's because he learned from a little bird—
Never talk to strangers!